Hands Up!

by **Breanna J. McDaniel** • illustrated by **Shane W. Evans**

Dial Books for 🏛 Young Readers

Greet the sun, bold and bright!

Tiny hands up!

Peek-a-boo—
hands up!

"Morning, baby.
Time to get dressed, hands up."

Stretch high!
Almost there, hands up.

Gotta get clean.
Reach for the sink, hands up.

"C'mon, little one, dry your tears.
Here, hold the bun, hands up."

Ready for takeoff, hands up!

"Please pick me, Ms. B!
Got my hands up!"

Adventure books live up top.
Reach high, tippy toes, hands up!

Graceful like Ms. Misty.
Fifth position, **hands up.**

Racing fast,
wind whistling,
hands up . . .

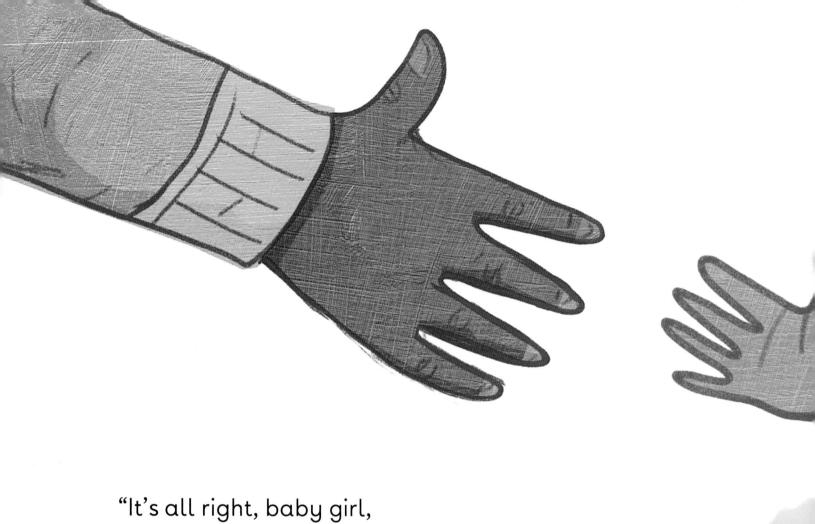

"It's all right, baby girl,
I'll help, **hands up.**"

The music flows through us.
"Aaaa-may-zi-in' grace!"
In praise and worship, **hands up!**

On the court fired up, jump ball, hands up . . .

"For the win, defense, hands up!"

On top of the world,
trophy to the sky, **hands up!**

We begin small, but we grow big.
Together we are mighty.
High fives all around, **hands up!**

SPREAD LOVE
NINGÚN SER HUMANO ES ILEGAL
WATER =LIFE
OVE YOUR NEIGHBOR